For information address Disney Press,
1101 Flower Street, Glendale, California 91201.

ISBN 978-1-4847-2082-0
FAC-023680-18211
3 5 7 9 10 8 6 4

For more Disney Press fun, visit www.disneybooks.com
This book was printed on paper created from a sustainable source.

# DISNEY
## MICKEY & FRIENDS

# DONALD TAKES A TRIP

**BOOK TWO**

New York • Los Angeles

It was a hot summer day. Mickey Mouse and his friends were relaxing in his living room. The friends were just deciding what to do with their day when *pop!* Mickey's air-conditioning broke!

"Maybe there will be a breeze outside," said Minnie.

But there was no breeze. Just nice, cool lemonade from Mickey's refrigerator.

"What are we going to do now?" asked Daisy.

Minnie looked around. "Hmmm . . ." she said. "Maybe we could make fans. Or we could try sitting in the shade under the tree. . . ."

"Gosh! Those sprinklers look nice and cool!" said Goofy, pointing down at Mickey's lawn.

Donald nodded. "But there isn't enough water coming out of them to keep us cool!" he said.

As Donald watched his friends looking at the sprinklers, he suddenly had an idea. "Let's go to the lake!" he shouted. "There's always a breeze there, and there's so much to do!"

"What a great idea!" said Mickey.

"It *is* the perfect day for a swim," Daisy added.

Donald and his friends piled into Mickey's car. In no time, they were on their way. As they drove, they sang songs and played games. They were so excited for their day at the lake!

When they arrived, the friends jumped into the water.

"Aah," said Mickey. The water felt nice on the very hot day.

Minnie leaned back and closed her eyes. "You were right, Donald. This *was* a good idea!"

Soon the friends had cooled off.

"What should we do now?" asked Minnie.

Everyone had a different idea. Daisy wanted to play basketball. Mickey and Pluto wanted to play Frisbee. And Donald wanted to go fishing!

Before anyone could stop him, Donald raced off
toward a little boat docked beside the water.

"Wait up, Donald!" Minnie called. "I don't think we can all fit in the boat. Why don't we do something together?"

But Donald only wanted to go fishing. He didn't care about spending time with his friends. Jumping in his boat, he rowed out to the middle of the lake.

At last, he found a good spot. Donald slowed his boat. Then, happily, he dropped his fishing line in the water.

Donald waited.

And he waited.

But his fishing line never moved!

Donald was getting upset. The lake was very quiet
and boring all by himself. And where were the fish?
Then he heard a splashing noise.

Donald turned around and saw a fish!
He heard another splash and turned again.

The fish kept splashing,
and Donald kept turning!

Soon Donald was all tangled up.

Just then, Goofy swam by.

"Gosh," he said. "You look like you could use

some help!"

Goofy untangled Donald. Then he climbed aboard the boat and the friends fished together.

Donald was glad to have Goofy along. It turned out, fishing was more fun with a friend!